Rumpelstiltskin

Fairy Tale Treasury

Adapted by
Jane Jerrard

Illustrations by
Burgandy Nilles

Publications Internatio

Long ago, there lived a poor miller and his beautiful daughter. The miller was a silly man who could not keep from bragging. One day, he was lucky enough to meet the King, and he bragged that his daughter could spin straw into gold.

The King, even though he was already rich, always wanted more gold. So he had the girl come to his castle that very day.

That night, when the little man asked gleefully if the Queen had any guesses left unguessed, she said, "Perhaps you are…

RUMPELSTILTSKIN?"

At the sound of his name, the little man grew so angry that he stamped his feet until he stamped himself right through the floor! And that was the last ever seen of Rumpelstiltskin.

All that night, the Queen sat up and made a list of every name she knew. Then she sent a servant out to discover new names she had not heard before.

When the little man returned the next evening, the Queen called out names one at a time.

But at each name, the little man just smiled and shook his head.

The second day, the servant came back with the strangest names in the whole kingdom. When the little man appeared that night, the Queen called him by each name. But he only shook his head.

The third day, the servant returned with no names at all, but he told the Queen a strange story: He had seen an odd little man dancing around a campfire, singing that RUMPELSTILTSKIN was his name.

When the miller's daughter arrived, the King led her to a little room filled with straw. He gave her a spinning wheel and told her to spin all the straw into gold by morning and he would make her Queen. As soon as he left, the poor girl started to cry, for she had no idea how to make straw into gold.

Suddenly the door flew open, and there stood a funny little man, no higher than her waist!

The girl told him about her impossible task.

"Well, I can spin straw into gold," said the little man. "But what will you give me for my work?"

"You may have my necklace," said the girl.

And so the little man set to work, and by morning he had spun every bit of straw into gold.

The next morning, the King was amazed to see the gold. But he did not marry the miller's daughter. Instead, he took her to a much larger room filled with straw and told her to spin it into gold. The poor girl, left all alone again, began to cry.

The door opened and there again stood the little man! He told her he would turn the straw to gold in return for her ring. And he spun every bit of straw into gold.

The next day, the King led the miller's daughter to a third room filled with straw. There she waited for the strange little man. But when he arrived the girl had nothing left to give him.

"Give me your first child when you become Queen," he said.

The girl agreed, for she did not believe she would ever be Queen. But the next day, when the King saw the room filled with gold, he finally did marry her.

A year later, the King and Queen had a beautiful baby. The Queen had forgotten all about the little man. But the first day she held her new baby, he appeared before her and asked for the child.

The Queen wept and begged to keep her baby. Feeling sorry for her, the little man told her she could have three days and nights to guess his name. If she guessed right, she could keep her child.